RURAL

RODEO
princess

M.G. Higgins

SADDLEBACK
EDUCATIONAL PUBLISHING

Gravel Road

SADDLEBACK
EDUCATIONAL PUBLISHING
www.sdlback.com

ISBN-13: 978-1-68021-061-3
ISBN-10: 1-68021-061-0
eBook: 978-1-63078-377-8

Printed in Guangzhou, China
NOR/0515/CA21500667

19 18 17 16 15   1 2 3 4 5

Chapter 1

Freddie tosses his head. Prances. I know he'd like to go full out. I pat his neck. "Not now, boy. Barrel drills tomorrow. I promise."

Today, it's endurance. Building his stamina. The goal is Evans Lake. Thirty miles round trip.

The wind picks up behind me. Goes right through my fleece jacket. I twist in the saddle. Dark clouds are building. Another storm? It's late April. This Montana winter is lasting forever. I squeeze my legs. Urge Freddie to a brisk walk. His hooves splatter through muddy snowmelt.

We get to Rattlesnake Hill. It borders the McNair ranch. I could go around it. But I pull Freddie to a stop. Take a moment to decide. Realize the decision was made when I came this way in the first place.

I turn his head toward the narrow cattle trail. I don't have to ask. He takes it at a trot. Zigzags to the top. He's so loyal. Such a willing accomplice. We get to the peak. He's breathing hard. So am I. But not from exertion.

Below us lies the McNair ranch. Two-story log cabin mansion. Stable bigger than our double-wide trailer. Covered riding arena. Fenced and cross-fenced pastures. About fifty quarter horses that I can see. Someone is lunging a palomino in an outdoor arena. Too far away to tell exactly who it is. Too short and thin for Mr. McNair. Probably one of his hands. Or a new trainer. They're always hiring new trainers. The ones raved about in horse magazines.

I'm about to pull Freddie around when I see movement. Under the roof of the covered arena. Horse's legs. Red boots. A smooth canter. Could be Amy McNair. Or her mom. Or one of Amy's friends. She's quickly out of sight again. I could wait for another glance. Decide against it. I'm not that desperate.

I click my tongue. Freddie scurries down the hill. We're soon back on the trail. To hell with taking it easy. I loosen the reins. Give him his head. The wind whips my face. We sprint a good ways. I slow him down. Ask myself if that glimpse of my former life was worth it. I don't feel any better for it. So, no. It wasn't.

We get to Evans Lake. The clouds are almost overhead now. Dark. Stormy. Snow in them, for sure. The temperature has dropped several more degrees. Damn. I could have sworn it was spring this morning. I should have checked the weather report. It was stupid of me not to.

I turn Freddie. Fifteen miles to home. I don't want to

push him. But I have to. I'm not dressed for snow. He willingly speeds up. He wants to get to his oat bucket as much as I want him there.

Bits of falling ice prick my face. Then thick, wet flakes. I urge Freddie to a gallop.

Halfway home and it's a full-on blizzard. Can't see more than a few feet ahead. I tug the reins. Just as I do, Freddie trips. Goes down on a knee. I barely stay in the saddle. Right away he's up again. Walking. I should stop him. Check his legs. But he's not limping. And I'm really cold. Too cold. I didn't even think to bring gloves.

I pull my hat down tight. Wrap the reins around the saddle horn. Slip my hands under my arms to keep them warm. Let Freddie use his instincts. Guide us home.

I can just make out our stable's blue roof. I'm shivering. My teeth are chattering. I slide off. Lead Freddie inside. Quickly take off his saddle and bridle. Make sure he has water and hay. I'll have to brush him later. I need to get inside. Need to get warm.

We never heat the double-wide more than sixty-five degrees to save money. But the kitchen feels blessedly warm compared to outside. I rush to my bedroom. Change out of my wet clothes. Throw on a jacket. Wrap a blanket around my shoulders. I'm still shivering. Back in the kitchen I make a pot of coffee. Sit at the table. Hunch my shoulders. Clasp the hot mug between my palms.

The house is empty. Is it possible my dad and brothers are out looking for me? No. I left early this morning. None of them was up yet. I didn't leave a note. They wouldn't have known where I was.

I look out the window. The snow has stopped. I should get back to the stable. Take care of Freddie and the other horses. But the cold has seeped deep into my bones. I feel frozen. Like I'll never move again.

The door bangs open. Dad barges in. Followed by my two older brothers. They wipe their muddy boots on the mat. Toss their coats onto the hooks near the door. They fill the kitchen.

"Where were you off to this morning?" Dad asks.

"Gave Freddie a ride," I answer.

He grabs a beer from the fridge. "Did you get stuck in that storm?"

"Yeah."

"That came out of nowhere. You okay?"

"Just cold. Where were you?" I ask.

"In town."

My brothers grab beers too. "Hey, what's for dinner?" Toby asks me.

I glance at the clock. Can't believe it's five already. "I don't know." I shrug the blanket off my shoulders. Nothing warms me up like the male members of my family. They're better than a furnace.

"Soon, okay?" Seth says. "We're going out again."

They disappear down the hall. I set my coffee cup on the table. Stare at it a second longer. Pull myself up. Search through cupboards. Find canned stew in the pantry. Heat it on the stove. Peel a few carrots. Toss a box of crackers on the counter. Dinner is fixed in ten minutes. They're done eating it ten minutes later.

Toby and Seth stride to the back door.

"You're leaving *now*?" I say. "What about Mom?"

They glance at each other. Shrug their shoulders. Seth says, "Tell her hi for us."

"Tell her yourself! You can't wait a few minutes?" Then I see Dad is joining them. "You too?" I say.

"We're going to the basketball game. Garth's son is playing. Saw him in town. Promised we'd go. Cheer for his kid." He runs his hand over his bald head. "Tell her … I miss her. Okay?"

They're out the door. The kitchen is empty again. The temperature drops a few degrees.

Chapter 2

I wash the dishes. Start the computer. Open Skype. Mom calls every Saturday. As close to six as she can. But plans don't always go the way you want. Not in the military. Not a million miles away in Afghanistan.

I know that's one reason the rest of my family bailed. Sometimes we wait forever. Then the connection is bad. Or there's nothing to say. That, and Garth will treat everyone to drinks at the 77 Bar after the game.

It's about six fifteen when the call comes in. Early morning halfway around the world. There she is. In her desert camo uniform. Kind face. Dark hair flattened by headphones. She smiles. "Hi, Jade."

"Hi, Mom." I push back tears. Know the army would tell us if something bad happened. But it's always such a relief to see her. Hear her voice.

"How are you?" she asks.

"I'm good. How are you?"

"Not too bad. Tired."

"When are you coming home?" I feel like such a little kid when I say it.

"Nothing's changed. Still looks like September. Where are the boys?"

"Basketball game."

"Basketball? Since when?" She looks annoyed.

"I don't know. Something about Garth's kid. Seth says hi. Dad says he misses you."

She rolls her eyes.

"We had a blizzard today," I say. "Freddie and I got caught in it."

"Honey, are you okay?" She looks worried. Mom would have come looking for me. If she'd been here. She also would have been up before I left. Cooked me breakfast. Reminded me to check the weather. Take my gloves. Wear a heavier jacket.

"I'm fine," I say. "Freddie got us home."

"Good. Give him a pat for me. How's school?"

I shrug.

"Jade," she says. "I know the rodeo's coming up. But you can't ignore your schoolwork."

"It would help if I didn't have so much work around here. If Seth and Toby would lift a finger to help."

She sighs.

"Can't you say something to them?"

"We've talked about this," she says. "I'm not there.

You're the woman of the house. If something has to give, it's the horses. Have you been going to church?"

I don't answer.

"Go tomorrow," she says. "How's Mike?"

"Fine."

She smiles. "Good." She looks over her shoulder. "I have to go, honey. Take care of yourself. Give my love to the boys. I expect to see them next week."

"I'll tell them."

"I love you."

"I love you too."

I kiss my fingers. Press them to the screen. She does the same. A final smile. And she's gone. I'm left with the same sense I always have. That she ended the call sooner than she needed to.

I turn off the computer. Throw on my field coat. Go to the stable. Feed the horses. Brush Freddie. Wipe the fur that's still wet. I rub my hand down his left foreleg. I think it's the one that buckled earlier. It feels fine. I feel his right leg.

No. Oh no.

His ankle is hot to the touch. Swollen.

No, no, no.

I lean my forehead against his shoulder. Go back in the house. Call Doc Dot. Leave a message for her to call me.

৯

I long ago lost the belief that church has the answers to

everything. But I go the next morning. It's important to Mom. And I'm thinking a prayer for Freddie couldn't hurt.

My dad and brothers aren't up when I leave. They came home pretty late. They're out late most Fridays and Saturdays now. Mom was our anchor. Now they're slowly floating away.

I sit next to my friend Lily and her family. Pastor Nichols preaches from the Bible. About how God forgives people. But forgiveness only applies to certain people. And I'm not one of them. I worship along with everyone else anyway. As if all of this applies to me. In case it does, I ask God to heal Freddie.

After the service, Lily and I lean against her SUV in the parking lot. Wait for her parents. I tell her about Freddie.

"You're kidding me," she says. "You've trained him since he was born."

"I never should have gone out yesterday."

"You didn't know there'd be a freak storm."

I shrug.

"So what are you going to do about the barrel race?"

"I have to cancel. I don't have another horse ready."

"Jade!" People stare at Lily as they walk to their cars. "You can't," she says more softly. "You're the best."

"I don't have a choice."

"I wish I had a horse to loan you. What about Amy?"

"A McNair horse?" I laugh. "No way."

"I know you guys aren't friends anymore. But this is an emergency. Without you, there's no competition. I bet even Amy would agree with that."

"Maybe Freddie's leg isn't that bad," I say.

৵

Veterinarian Dorothy Miller, Doc Dot, arrives that afternoon. She tells me Freddie has a sprain. "Keep him isolated," she says. "It will heal on its own. No riding. And certainly no barrel racing. Not until I give the okay." She leaves me with care instructions.

I walk back to the house. Hold back tears. I'm glad it wasn't any worse than a sprain. But I was hoping it was nothing. That maybe God heard me. Thought me worthy of a miracle.

I wanted to win this race. I came in second last year. Missed first to Amy McNair by a tenth of a second. I'm a better rider now. I've been training every chance I get. Every bit of spare time.

And Freddie was coming along. He's fast. Smart. Powerful. Good instincts. Everything you want in a barrel racer. We could have done it. Winning the Wyatt annual rodeo would have set me up for going to the next level.

I think about Lily's suggestion. About borrowing one of Amy's horses. She always has at least three ready to go. Depending on the type of race. The weather. Her mood. The horses' moods. The color of her outfit. She told me once her horses are worth fifty to one hundred grand each. Freddie cost practically nothing. We bred my mare Misty to another neighbor's quarter horse. I've done all the training.

There are too many reasons why using one of Amy's horses is a bad idea. So I push the thought out of my head.

Chapter 3

I'm up at four thirty Monday morning. Grateful it's a fraction warmer. Grateful the sun is up a fraction earlier. I do my horse chores. Brush Freddie, even though I don't have the time. Feed him a carrot.

My family is up at six. At least they haven't floated so far they've given up working the ranch. I fix them breakfast. Try to keep a good attitude. Remind myself Mom will be home in five months.

I start the forty-five-minute drive to school in my pickup. Notice I'm almost out of gas. Pull off the highway when I get to Wyatt. A banner announcing the sixty-fourth Wyatt annual rodeo stretches across Main Street. I quickly look away. Pull into Smitty's garage. Jump out of the truck to pump gas. Mr. Price lifts his head from under the hood of an SUV. Nods in my direction.

"Hi, Mister Price." I give him a small wave. I've been dating his son, Mike, since October. I still don't know if he accepts me in Mike's life. I think it's mainly because of my brothers. They aren't exactly upstanding citizens. They've been arrested for drunk driving. Disorderly conduct. I've never gotten into trouble. Doesn't matter. Lots of people think I'm the same as them. I'm a Dobbs.

I get to school late. Slip into first-period English. Mr. Lynch glances at me. Doesn't say anything. Unlike other teachers, he's cool. He knows what I'm dealing with at home. Cuts me some slack.

The period ends. Mike waits for me outside the classroom. Smiles. Wraps his arm around my shoulders. "Hey," he says.

"Hey."

We walk down the hall toward math. Wyatt Junior-Senior High School's most unlikely couple. He's a townie. Smart. College-bound. I'm a ranch kid. Not all that smart. Nowhere-bound.

"How did your endurance ride go?" he asks.

"Not great." I tell him about getting stuck in the blizzard. About Freddie's sprain.

Mike looks away.

"What?" I ask.

"Why didn't you call me?"

"There's nothing you could have done."

He pulls his arm away. "Maybe. But that must have been scary. I could have empathized. I could have cried with you. Did you cry?"

I smile. "No. But I wanted to." Mike is also good at trying to cheer me up. Why I didn't call him?

"Wait." He stops in the hallway. Kids flow around us. "Freddie's hurt! First of all, I feel bad for the big guy. Please give him my regards. But what about the rodeo?"

"I'll have to drop out."

"No!" He grips my wrist. "Jade. You've been looking forward to this like forever. All that training. All those weekends when we could have been together. There must be another option. What about Misty?"

"Right." Misty is older than me. She's also slow. Mike rode her once, so he knows this. "We'd better get to class."

He sighs. "Fine. I brought Mom's cookies for lunch. Maybe they'll make you feel better."

"Chocolate chip?"

"Snickerdoodles."

"You're mom is awesome. And you really *are* my favorite boyfriend."

"I love it when you say that." He kisses my cheek. "It's such a turn-on."

Ms. Kline reads the daily announcements. She ends with, "And congratulations to Amy McNair, Claire Ward, and Samantha Davis. This year's Wyatt annual rodeo princesses!" She sets down the paper and claps.

The three of them are in class today. Students cheer. This is not a big surprise. They're the prettiest girls in school. I'm sure they all expected it. I don't glance in Amy's direction. Don't want to see the smug look on her face. Though I never glance in her direction anyway. No reason to start now.

୬

I head to one of the cottonwood trees at lunch. It's where I hang out. As long as it's not too wet. Mike thinks I'm a loner. But it's because of Amy and her friends. Who also used to be my friends. I don't like being around any of them.

Mike joins me. Scarfs down his sandwich. "A really cool James Cameron movie starts this Friday. Want to come?"

He works at the Roxy, Wyatt's only movie theater. He gets me in for free. I'm not a huge movie fan. But I'm not training for the rodeo now. The distraction might be nice. "Sure. That would be great."

"Awesome. Here." He hands me two snickerdoodles. Jumps to his feet. "I promised Mister Welker I'd help him set up the bio lab."

"Don't break anything. Microscopes are expensive."

"Are you kidding me? I've got my non-klutz superpowers today." He walks away and pretends to trip.

I laugh. My smile fades. I lower my eyes. Break off a chunk of cookie. Crumble it in my fingers.

"Jade?"

My heart skips a beat. I look up. Blonde hair. Rosy cheeks. Green eyes. Full red lips.

Amy.

I look down again. Battle my stomach. Curling. Rising. Free-falling.

"Jade!" she repeats. Annoyed.

I get myself under control. "Hi. Congrats on being rodeo princess."

"Thanks. I hear you need a barrel horse."

Lily must have told her. I wish she hadn't.

"I'm going to win," Amy says. "Whether you race or not. Which means I don't really give a crap. But I want to post a good time. I need someone to compete against. Unfortunately, that's you. Do you want to borrow a horse?"

Don't really give a crap. I want to slap her. But I want to barrel race more. "Maybe," I say.

"I haven't cleared it with my parents," she says. "I'll let you know." She walks back to her friends Claire, Dana, and Tyler. They walk into the building. Probably to go to the restroom to check their makeup. The bell's about to ring.

I get up. Brush dirt off my butt. Two weeks isn't much time to train on a new horse. It will take a lot of work. I'll have to trailer it to my ranch. Take care of it, along with the other horses. On top of everything else I have to do. But I'll make it work. I want this. I want to win. I want to beat Amy McNair. And to do it on one of her horses? Yes. That would be very nice.

Chapter 4

That night I get a text message from Amy. "Ok to borrow Dilly. But u need to ride her here. Dad paranoid. Might be best if u bail."

I read the text three times. Her dad is paranoid? Of what? That I might hurt his precious horse? Steal her? Amy doesn't want me there? I force myself not to throw the phone across the room. Text back, "I'll start tomorrow."

The phone rings. It's Amy. "Hey," I say.

"Hey. Look. I'm not so sure about this."

"You made the offer. Are you taking it back?"

Silence. Then, "I need to practice too."

I roll my eyes. "I'll stay in the outdoor arena. Our paths won't cross."

More silence. Then a sigh. "Talk to Jesse when you get here. He's one of our new ranch hands. He'll get Dilly for you."

"I can get her myself. Just describe her to me."

"No," Amy says quickly. "It's an insurance thing.

That's why you can't trailer her to your place. Dad is firm about it."

"Okay. Fine. Thanks."

She clicks off.

҂

I tell Mike at lunch the next day.

"Dilly," he says. "Sounds like a pickle. Not a horse."

"Like Misty sounds like a horse? Or Freddie?"

He shrugs. "True. If I had a horse, I'd name her"—he pauses dramatically—"Horsey."

I pick up his hand. Stroke his fingers. "I'll be training until the rodeo. Afternoons and weekends. You won't be seeing much of me."

"So no movie this weekend?"

"No. Sorry."

He makes a sad face. "Boohoo. So basically the next two weeks will be like the past month."

"Pretty much."

"Well, we always have school," he says with a gravelly voice. "And the cottonwood tree." He leans in. Kisses me. I kiss him back. His lips are soft. His kiss gentle. Tentative. He must wonder why I let him kiss me at lunch. In the open. When I push him away when we're alone.

It's because I want Amy, Claire, Dana, and Tyler to see this. I want the gossipers to talk. I want my brothers to hear. And my mom and dad. And Pastor Nichols. And other members of Grace Evangelical. "Jade and Mike," I want the gossipers to say. Maybe with a wink. A sly smile. "They're all over each other. They seem pretty serious."

He pulls away first. "Wow." He's breathing heavily. "I'd better stop. The bell's going to ring."

He looks at me with gooey eyes. He's in deep. I would give anything for my heart to be pounding right now. The way I know his is. He's such a good person. A kind person. I tell myself I'm practice for him. In a year he'll go to college. Move on to someone else. He won't be a complete newbie. He'll thank me for this. Remember me fondly.

That's what I tell myself.

"Have I told you lately how incredible you are?"

"You just did," I say.

"Well, have I told you lately that I really like you?"

"You just did."

"Okay. Just so you know," he says.

"I know."

He gives me a loopy grin. "I'm incredible too. Right?"

"Of course."

He nods. The bell rings. "Civics. Can't wait." He gets to his feet. Pulls me up. "Let's go be civil." He wraps his arms around my waist. We head to class.

Amy walks ahead of us in the hallway. Troy Regan is with her. Her boyfriend since ninth grade. They're holding hands. Wear matching silver purity rings.

Amy and Troy. Beautiful. Perfect. They remind me of two teacups. Unbroken. Unchipped. Like the ones my grandma kept in her china cabinet. Sometimes I'm tempted to take a hammer to them.

ᕲ

I drive home. Grab my boots. Saddle. Other tack. Throw it all in the back of the pickup. Climb in the cab. Remember something. Run back to the kitchen. Take a carrot from the fridge. Remember something else. Write a note: "At McNairs' ranch. Dinner will be late. Make a sandwich if you're hungry. Please."

The McNairs are our next-door neighbors. But it's still a fifteen-minute drive. I get this weird déjà vu feeling. It's been over three years since I was last here. The summer before eighth grade. I wasn't driving yet. Well, not legally driving. I'd ride one of my horses. Usually Misty. Take a shortcut through our pastures. It took less time than driving.

I head down the long gravel driveway. My heart beats a little faster. This was my second home. My second family. I see the McNairs in town every once in a while. Or at school. They're always nice. Polite. But I'm not sure what to expect. I never found out what Amy told them. About why we were best friends one day. And enemies the next.

I drive by the house. Where I ate so many meals. Spent so many nights in Amy's room. I park near the stable. A guy meanders out. Steps over to my truck. Young. Tall. Tight jeans. Red-checkered shirt. Handsome face that dimples when he smiles. "Hi," he says.

"Hi." I get out of the truck. "You Jesse?"

"You must be Jade Dobbs."

I reach for my saddle.

"Want me to get that?" he asks.

"No. I'm good."

He walks with me to the stable. "Jade. That's a pretty name. You named after that green stone?"

"I don't know. Never asked. Jesse. That's an interesting name. You named after Jesse James?"

"I don't know." He laughs. "Never asked."

I stop in the tack room. Set my saddle on a saddle stand.

"I'll bring Dilly around," he says. Jesse walks down the wide sawdust corridor. Ten large stalls on either side. That's just this wing. Huge compared to my four-stall stable. Everything is like I remember. Neat. Clean. Shiny buckets and oiled tack sit outside every stall. Groomed quarter horses stick their heads over their gates.

I spent countless hours here with Amy. Brushing horses. Saddling horses. Talking about horses. It was who we were. What we did. Horse crazy. I still am. Just in a different way. A more serious way.

Jesse leads a dapple-gray toward me. She's beautiful. Perfect conformation. Well muscled. Her ears perk forward.

I pull the carrot out of my pocket.

Jesse sees the treat and holds up his hand. "Nope. Sorry. They're on strict diets."

"Of course they are." I shove the carrot back in my pocket. Pet Dilly's nose.

"I know. It's crazy." He lowers his voice. "Their trainer is wacky if you ask me. But I just work here."

I saddle and bridle Dilly. Jesse chats at me the whole time. Seems he's twenty-one. Been here a few months. He's a bull rider. Saving money. Planning to join the rodeo circuit at some point. "For now I'm just happy to have a job," he says.

There's a noise at the other end of the stable. Amy. She just a silhouette in the bright doorway. But I know it's her. I will always know it's her.

Chapter 5

Jesse beams at the sight of Amy. His smile just about breaks his face. "Gotta go," he says to me. "Boss's daughter."

"Right," I say. "Thanks."

He politely tugs the brim of his hat. Strides through the stable. He's not hurrying because he has to. He wants to. I wonder if Mr. Perfect Troy Regan knows someone has a crush on his girlfriend.

I throw the bridle hard over Dilly's neck. She bobs her head. "Sorry," I murmur. I remind myself I'm here to train. So I can win a race. That's all. I'm going to avoid Amy. Because she asked me to. Because that's what I need to do. Want to do. I don't care about her love life. It means nothing to me.

I lead Dilly to the outdoor arena. The barrels are freshly painted. Perfectly set. The dirt is raked smooth. For a second I'm flattered. Think maybe it's for me. But it's for the horses, of course. To lessen the chance of injury.

I ride Dilly around the arena. Get to know her. Let her get to know me. She has a nice walk. Smooth trot and canter. She's responsive. Sensitive. I love Freddie. I trained him. He's my horse in every way. But Dilly's top breeding shows.

I do some drills. Circles. Then figure eights. Slow at first. Then faster. She flies. Still has more speed to give.

I finish another figure eight. Pat her neck.

"Hey!"

I look over. Amy's sitting on a bay gelding. Just outside the corral. Her posture is a little slouched. Like she didn't just ride up a second ago. She's been watching me.

I ride Dilly closer. But not too close. "What?"

"I think you've practiced enough today. Don't wear her out."

"She's not worn out. But if you want me to go, I will."

We both turn at the sound of tires on gravel. A giant SUV rolls to a stop. Sally McNair emerges from inside. Sky blue pantsuit. White silk blouse. Blonde hair set in a shoulder-length flip. Half a can of hairspray holding it in place. Most people think she's as stuck-up as her hair. But it's all for show. She has a big heart. I've always liked her.

She floats over to us. Flashes a huge grin. "Jade!"

"Hi, Mrs. McNair."

"I was thrilled when Amy said you'd be coming. I'm so glad you've patched things up. I've missed you. So has

Amy. Although she won't admit it. Stubborn, like her dad. But you know that."

I glance at Amy. She's looking across the arena. Her face a blank mask.

"Can you stay for dinner?" Mrs. McNair asks.

"No," Amy says for me. "She told me she has plans." Amy gives me a subtle glare.

"Right," I say. "I have to get home."

"Well, another night this week, then. How about Wednesday? We'll have ribs. And custard pie. Are they still your favorites?"

I haven't had either of those in over three years. Since I was last here. I can taste those sweet ribs melting in my mouth. The creamy, rich pie. I shouldn't. I know that. But it's like I've ridden Freddie up to the base of Rattlesnake Hill. I have no choice. I have to ride to the top. "That would be great. Thanks."

Mrs. McNair looks from me to Amy. Smiles wistfully. Sadly. "It's so good seeing you two together. It's like you're thirteen again." She turns for the house.

Now I'm sad. The last three years were my fault. At least, I think they were.

"Why did you do that?" Amy hisses. "Jade, we had an agreement."

"Sorry. She asked. I didn't want to be rude."

"You'd better go now," Amy says. "Jesse will take care of Dilly for you."

"Is it okay if I leave my tack here?"

She doesn't answer. Trots her horse to the covered arena.

I lead Dilly to the stable. Unsaddle her. Throw my saddle on a rack. Jesse's not around. I fish in my pocket. Feed Dilly the carrot before he comes back.

⁊

"What am I supposed to think?" Dad shouts. I've just walked into the kitchen. "We get home from working all day. Look forward to dinner. And all that's here is a note?"

I rummage in the fridge. Pull out some steaks. "You know how to make sandwiches."

"Of course we know how to make sandwiches! Sandwiches are for lunch. This is dinner."

"Okay! I'm fixing it now." I start peeling potatoes.

He takes a beer from the fridge.

"Dad?" I say before he heads to the living room. "I'm eating dinner at the McNairs' on Wednesday. I'll fix you something before I go. You'll just have to heat it up."

He grunts. Leans against the doorjamb. I feel him staring at me. "You two get over your tiff?"

"They're letting me borrow one of their horses. For the rodeo."

"Will wonders never cease." He pops the can. Slurps. "I hear you and the Price kid have been necking at school."

I roll my eyes. The Wyatt gossip mill is working.

"Are you using protection?" he asks.

I glare at him. "Dad!"

"Your mom's not here. Someone has to bring it up. She'll blame me if you get knocked up while she's away."

"I'm not going to get *knocked up*."

Seth has joined Dad in the doorway. "Why not?" He crosses the kitchen to the fridge.

I lower my eyes.

"Why not, Jade? Why won't you get knocked up?"

"Hey," Dad scolds him. "What's with you?"

Seth gives me a long stare. Leaves with a beer.

"What the hell was that about?" Dad asks me.

"I don't know." I focus on the potatoes. "He's Seth."

Dad stands there a second longer. Leaves.

I close my eyes. Take a deep breath. Set the pot of potatoes on the stove.

Chapter 6

I finish making dinner. We eat. I wash dishes. Take care of the horses. Check Freddie's leg. It's still swollen. Not as much as before. I'm glad.

It's eight thirty by the time I shower. Collapse at my desk. I've got a ton of homework. But I just want to sleep. I look wistfully at my bed. My alarm will be blaring me awake in eight hours.

I feel a presence in the doorway. Seth leans against the jamb. I wonder if he's trying to look like Dad. Or if hulking comes naturally to the men in my family. "I saw something on TV the other day," he says.

I return to my homework. "Good for you."

"About being gay," he says.

I stare at my math book. Force myself to stay calm.

"These experts were saying you're born with it. There's nothing you can do to change. Is that true?"

"Why are you asking me?"

"You know why."

I look up. Meet his eyes. "I'm not gay."

"It's a sin. That's what Pastor Nichols says."

"How would you know? You hardly go to church."

He shrugs. "I'm glad you're with Mike. I really am. Even though he's a townie. And a twerp. It's the right thing to do. For you and our family. I was just wondering how hard it is. If you think about girls when you're with him."

I glare at my brother. "I. Am. Not. Gay. Get out of my room. I have to study."

"Sure." He leaves. Turns back. "You're my sister, Jade. I care about you. I want you to be happy."

"I'm happy. Don't worry about me." I jump up. Shut the door on him. Sit at my desk. Grip the corners of my text-book. Force them into my palms. More and more. Until all I'm aware of is the pain.

ⴢ

Tuesday I go to the McNair ranch straight from school. Jesse is his usual chatty self. I have to drag Dilly away from him. Want to get in as much practice as I can. She's skittish today. A little uncooperative. I need to learn her moods. Or maybe she needs to learn mine. Thankfully, I don't see Amy.

Wednesday after school I make the boys a tuna casserole. Leave a note on how to heat it. Hope between the three of them they can figure it out. I work with Dilly for an hour. Just an easy trail ride today. I want this to be fun. Want her to look forward to seeing me.

No one has to tell me when dinner is. Dinner at the McNairs' is always at six. I wash my hands and face in the stable bathroom. Comb my hair. Change into the clothes I brought with me. A nice pair of jeans. A clean shirt. Dress boots. Head up to the house at five fifty.

The sun is setting. Warm lamplight shines out through the massive two-story front window. My heart flops as I step onto the broad wooden porch. It's been so long since I was here.

The door opens a second after I knock. "Jade! You don't have to knock. Come in." Robert McNair smothers me in a bear hug. He's tall. Big, but not fat. Hair graying at the temples. He lets me go. Squeezes my shoulders. "It's so good to see you." He says it like he means it.

"Hi," I say. "Thanks. It's good to be here." I say it like I mean it too. Because I do.

We walk into the barn-like living room. My boots echo on the wooden floor. The room hasn't changed much. Soft leather sofa and chairs. Chandelier made from antlers. Tall stone fireplace. Western paintings on the walls. The smell of barbecue wafts in from the kitchen.

"Too bad about your horse," Mr. McNair says. "How serious is it?"

"He'll be okay. The vet says it will take time."

"Hey, I'm sorry about the on-site rule. Darn lawyers and insurance agents. You know how it is."

I don't have the slightest idea *how it is*. But I nod and smile. "I'm grateful you're letting me ride Dilly. She's a great horse."

"Isn't she? Got her from a breeder in Texas. Made a sweet deal. She's worth a fortune. If you do well on her, it will up her price even more." He winks. Raises his chin and looks past me. "Ah, there she is."

Amy is walking down the stairs from the second floor. She's wearing a tight pink T-shirt. Black yoga pants. Blonde hair pulled back in a smooth ponytail. Heat flushes my face. I bite the inside of my cheek.

"Look who the cat dragged in," he says to her.

She doesn't say anything.

"So," Mr. McNair says. "I'm going to see how your mom and Marta are doing with dinner. Get us some drinks. You still like Coke?" he asks me.

"I can't believe you remember."

"Of course I remember!" He gives me another wink. Mom once said Robert McNair could charm the scales off a snake. Now that I'm older I get what she means.

Amy sinks into a soft chair. Stretches her legs out. Stares at her black slippers. I'm not sure what to do with myself. Maybe this wasn't such a good idea. We'll be sitting at the same table. Having to make conversation.

I just wanted … I'm not sure what I wanted. A good meal? One I didn't have to cook. With adults who care about me. Maybe I just wanted to be inside this house again. Remind myself what it's like to be part of a normal family.

I wander to the fireplace. Look at the painting of cows above the mantle. "Moo and Mack," I say with a smile.

Amy doesn't respond.

"That's what we named the cows in the painting. Remember? We went looking for them on my ranch. That's when you decided all cows look alike. Your mom was so mad when we came back. She'd been about to call Sheriff Becker. Thought we'd been kidnapped."

"This won't work," Amy says.

"What?"

"What you're doing right now. Trying to get back into my life."

"That's not what I'm doing," I say.

"You should have said no. That was the deal. You stay out of my life. I don't tell anyone what you are."

"I never wanted to stop being your friend."

"No, but I did. I thought you got that. I thought you respected that." She gets to her feet. "I decided a long time ago to forgive you, Jade. It's the Christian thing to do. Jesus says to love everyone. Even if what they've done is wrong. But I'm not going to put myself in that situation again. I've seen the look in your eyes. It makes my skin crawl. It's evil."

I wince. As though she slapped me. "It didn't make your skin crawl three years ago."

Her face turns red. "Get out," she hisses. "GET. OUT."

"Tell your parents I'm sorry. I'm sure you'll come up with a good excuse."

I walk to my truck. The tires spew gravel as I fly out of there.

Chapter 7

I slow down when I'm off McNair land. Grip the steering wheel. Fight the tears wanting to pour out. And the flooding memories. They both come anyway. It was the end of summer. We were out riding. Amy had been quiet all day. We got caught in a thunderstorm. Galloped our horses back to the stable. Toweled ourselves dry.

Amy started to cry. She sank into the corner of a stall. I sat next to her. She was sobbing. I kept asking, "What's wrong? What's wrong?"

She shook her head. Wouldn't answer.

I wrapped my arm around her. She leaned her head against my shoulder.

I don't remember who started it. First our eyes met. Then our lips. We were kissing. Everything suddenly fell into place. My life made sense. I didn't want to stop. She pulled away. Jumped up. "You'd better go," she said.

I hated leaving her. I wanted to talk about what had

just happened. Why she'd been crying. But I didn't want to upset her more. So I left.

I was a mess. I'd always known being attracted to girls was wrong. Heard Dad say hateful things about gay people. Mom was a firm believer in whatever Pastor Nichols preached. And he was definitely anti-gay. I'd hoped maybe it was a phase. I'd grow out of it. After kissing Amy, I knew better. It was not a phase. I was not normal.

Was Amy the same as me? Could I possibly be that lucky? Or had something else happened? I needed to see her again. Talk to her. But she'd been so upset. I wanted her to contact me first.

Eighth grade started a week later. I still hadn't heard from Amy. I met her in the morning at her locker. Just like always.

"We're not friends anymore," she said. Then she marched away. It was over. Just like that.

I didn't want to accept it. Later that day, I found her alone in the restroom. "Can we talk about this?" I said.

"No," she said. "Stay out of my life. Or I'll tell."

That was something I couldn't risk. I was certain my family would kick me out of the house. I had no place to go. I didn't know another gay person. Didn't know where to turn.

So I used the computer. Started going online. Looking at

forums. Trying to find kids like me. I found them. So did my brothers. I had no idea either of them knew about computers.

A year ago they found the computer's online history. Found the sites I'd visited. I told them I was doing a report for health class. They didn't believe me. They've been giving me hell ever since. Especially Seth.

The worst thing? I lost my best friend. And my second family. So many times I wished I could have taken back that kiss. Buried my feelings for her.

I still wish it. Was Amy right? Did I go there tonight wanting to get back into her life?

I get to the turnoff for our ranch. Stop the truck. Sit there. Pull out my phone. Think about calling Mike. Wish he was just a friend. But our relationship is too complicated. I could call Lily. She's a friend. But not a good-enough friend to discuss this. There's no one I can talk to.

I turn down our long driveway. Park near the stable. The moon is almost full. I throw on my field coat. Ride Misty bareback up Rattlesnake Hill. Sit there for the longest time. Stare at the warm light flowing through the windows of the McNair house. Imagine eating those delicious ribs. The custard pie. Mr. and Mrs. McNair asking about me. About my family. Caring about what I have to say.

I shake my head. Amy. The McNairs. They're like a drug. I can't do this to myself anymore. I'm not coming back here again. I turn Misty. Trot her home. I'm going to win that race. It's all I have.

୭

Amy doesn't make eye contact with me at school the next morning. Not that I expect her to. I swallow my pride. My anger. Text her, "Sorry about dinner. Want to keep training. Promise to keep my distance. Ok?"

It must take her a while to think about it. She doesn't text back until the afternoon. "Ok."

I drive out to the McNairs' ranch after school. Plan on spending an hour with Dilly, then going right home. Hope I don't run into Amy. Or her parents. I'm sure they're pissed at me for disappearing last night. Amy probably didn't go out of her way to make me look sympathetic.

I park near the stable. Walk inside. Hear voices. Mr. McNair and Jesse. I scoot into the tack room. Hope the conversation ends soon.

"Do you want to keep working here?" Mr. McNair's voice is loud. Harsh.

"Yeah. Sure." Jesse voice is defensive.

"Then do what I tell you. No more. No less. Do you understand?" He's slurring his words.

"Fine. I've got it."

"These horses are worth too much. Too goddamned much. I'll take it out of your pay. Then won't you be sorry. Mister Bull Rider. Mister Jesse Bull Rider."

Jesse doesn't respond. I hear a crash. "*Damn* it!" Mr. McNair swears.

Half a minute later, Jesse walks into the tack room. His cheeks are red. He jerks to a stop when he sees me. "Oh. Hey. Didn't know you were here." He takes his hat off. Nervously combs his fingers through his hair. "Did you hear any of that?"

"A little."

"I'm still not sure what I did wrong. I think he was drunk." He slips his hat back on. "You know this family. Is he like that very often?"

I shake my head. "He's usually really nice. Friendly."

"Yeah. Well. I won't put up with it. Life's too short." He looks over my shoulder. Like he's thinking about something. Then he smiles. "Guess you're here to ride Dilly. I'll get her."

I don't run into Amy that day. Or Friday. I'm relieved.

Chapter 8

The rodeo is in another week. Dilly and I are clicking. But I realize something when I train her with barrels. She has a bad habit of shouldering. Knocking barrels over. In a race, a tipped-over barrel is a five-second deduction. A sure loss.

Is this why Amy loaned her to me? She knows there's no way I'll win riding a horse that knocks barrels.

I'd been hoping I could limit training at this point. Stay away from the McNairs' as much as possible. But breaking Dilly's habit is going to take work. A lot of repetitions.

I'm up early on Saturday. I get to the stable about seven thirty. My intention is to avoid Amy. Jesse isn't there. I wonder if he has weekends off. Or if he just isn't up yet.

Now what? I'm supposed to let him get Dilly for me. I stand around a few minutes. This is stupid. I can get my own horse. I grab a brush from the tack room. Stride between the stalls. Notice horses are munching fresh hay. Someone has been here.

"Hello?" I call.

No answer.

I open the gate to Dilly's stall. "Hey, girl." She bobs her head. I stroke her neck. "Ready to work?"

"What are you doing?"

I turn. Amy. Dang. I want to disappear. "Jesse wasn't here," I say softly. "I didn't want to waste time."

"Well, that's the deal. Sorry."

I notice she's pushing a wheelbarrow. It's loaded with hay. I'm sure that's Jesse's job. Is she covering for him?

I set down my brush. Wait until she's in a stall. Then I head to the tack room to wait.

"Oh, go ahead," Amy says when I pass her. "Just don't let Dad catch you." She throws hay into the next stall. "Why are you here so early?"

I scoot back to Dilly. "Why do you think?"

"To avoid me. That didn't work out so well, did it?" She shoves the wheelbarrow.

I brush Dilly. Listen to hay landing with soft thuds. I decide to risk a question. "How long have you known Dilly has a shouldering problem?"

She's quiet a second. "Since we brought her home."

"You really despise me, don't you?" I brush Dilly hard. She snaps her head at me. "Sorry," I murmur.

"Yes. But Dilly was Dad's idea. He thinks you're a good rider. Thinks you might train her out of it."

I think of all the expensive trainers they pay for. "I don't know if I should be angry or flattered."

"Be anything you want." More hay thuds to the floor. "Jesse?!"

I turn. It's Mr. McNair. He is standing at the other end of the stable.

"Shoot," Amy mutters. She quickly opens a stall door. Whispers, "Don't tell him I'm here." She slides down.

Mr. McNair marches toward me. "Jesse!" he yells.

He gets even with Dilly's stall. Sees me. "Oh, Jade. It's you." He glances at the wheelbarrow. "Where's Jesse?"

"I don't know. He ran out a minute ago. Said he'd be right back."

"Would you tell him to come find me? By the way, you should let him do that."

"For insurance reasons?" I ask.

"Right. Hey, sorry about dinner the other night. Amy said you got sick. We missed you. Amy especially. She hardly said a word all night. I wish you two would straighten things out. She was a lot happier when you were friends."

I don't know what to say. So I don't say anything.

"So you'll tell Jesse to see me?" he says.

"Sure."

He marches out.

"Is he gone?" Amy whispers from her hiding spot.

"Yep."

She gets to her feet. Peers over the stall. "Thanks." She scrambles out. Slides behind the wheelbarrow again. "What my dad said wasn't true, you know. I didn't miss you at dinner. I was quiet for other reasons."

"Like what?" The question falls out of my mouth. It feels so natural to ask it. Especially between Amy and me. The old Amy and me.

"Stuff," she says, surprising me with an answer. "The school play. Rodeo princess. Barrel race. Some other things." She pauses. "It feels like I'm about to bust apart half the time." She throws hay into another stall. "So you and Mike Price. That's kind of weird."

I look at her.

"I thought you were, you know …"

Gay must be the word she's looking for. I bet she's been dying to ask me about him.

"You really like him?" she asks.

"Yes."

She nods. "Are you one of those? You know? You like both boys and girls?"

Damn her. Why are we talking? Why am I allowing it? I'm here to train. That's all. I don't answer. Finish brushing Dilly. Lead her out of the stall.

"I'm back!" Jesse sprints inside. He's panting. Sweating. Dilly shies as he passes. He comes back. Takes the lead rope from me. "Sorry. I'll do that."

"It's about time!" Amy says. "Dad came looking for you. He almost caught me."

"I got held up. I'm sorry." The next minute they're standing in front of each other. Smiling. He brushes a loose strand of hair behind her ear.

I head outside. Wait for Jesse to saddle Dilly. If Amy was still my friend, I'd ask her what's going on with Jesse. But she's not my friend. So I don't care.

I do a lot of drills with Dilly. Circles. Triangles. Figure eights. Ride around one barrel until she gets it right. Then move on to the next. Ride in the other direction. Hopefully she's remembering the good moves I'm teaching her. I decide to end with a short trail ride.

I turn us toward Beehive Trail. Amy and I made all the trails when we first started riding. Gave them silly names. This one loops around a mesa. We decided it looks like a beehive. I have to pass the covered arena to get there. Amy is riding her bay gelding. A woman I've never seen before barks instructions. Must be her trainer.

I should keep going. But I stop and watch. Check out my competition.

Amy lopes her horse into the alleyway. Gallops toward the first barrel. Rounds it. Does the next two. Then she's out again. Wow. She was fast. That's a really nice horse she'd riding. She sees me.

I brace myself for a frown. A snarl.

But she grins. Pumps her fist in the air with pure joy.

I smile back. Share that split second of joy with her. A split second of who we were.

Chapter 9

Dilly and I have been out maybe fifteen minutes. Galloping hoofbeats charge up behind us. Then Amy's riding next to me.

I tense. Stare straight ahead. Dilly flicks her ears.

"I want to talk to you about Jesse," Amy says. "What you think you saw in the stable. There's nothing going on between us. We're just friends."

I shrug.

"You won't tell Troy, will you?"

"Why would I?"

I figure she's delivered her message. She'll leave. But she says, "I watched you with Dilly today. You did better with her than her trainer. That guy was an idiot. I'm glad Dad fired him."

I shrug again.

"So how's your mom?" she asks. "I hear she's in Afghanistan. You must worry about her."

I pull Dilly to a stop. Stare at Amy. "Three days ago you ordered me to stay out of your life. You threatened me.

You said I was evil. Now you're chatting? Like nothing ever happened?"

"I didn't say *you* were evil. I said how you looked at me was evil."

"Right. Big difference."

"Fine." She turns her horse for the ranch.

My heart lurches. I'm confused. Still hurt from the things she's said to me. But she's reaching out. I can't ignore that. Can't ignore that moment of joy I felt a few minutes ago. I have so little joy in my life. "Amy. Wait." I turn Dilly. It's time to get back anyway.

I ride next to her. "Yes, my mom's in Afghanistan. I worry about her all the time."

"When's she coming home?"

"September."

"Are Seth and Toby still lazy pigs? Can't even pour their own water?"

I smile. "Yep."

"I can't imagine putting up with that. My mom is not my favorite person in the world. But I don't know what I'd do without her. Run away, probably."

"Really?"

She shrugs. We ride quietly for a few minutes. Lost in our own thoughts. Like we used to. When we were kids. Except we're not thirteen anymore. So much has changed. "Why are you talking to me, Amy?"

She stares straight ahead. "What my dad said to you earlier. That I was happier when we were friends. I've been thinking about it all morning. He's right. I haven't been happy in a long time. Things are so … complicated. I miss talking to you. I miss this. Riding together."

I've missed it too. So much. But I'm afraid to say it. Don't want her to take it the wrong way.

"So," Amy says. "I'm thinking if you keep your distance. You know, physical distance. And don't look at me weird. Maybe we can be friends again. What do you think?"

I think she's infuriating. I think she'll never understand who I am. She'll always think I'm evil. Sick. So, no. I don't want to be friends again. Yet I do. Desperately. She's Amy. I love her. I've always loved her. "Okay," I say softly.

"Cool. What do you think of Elvis?" She pats her horse's neck.

"He's fast."

She grins. "He's wicked fast. He's about the only thing I can count on lately. We're buds. Aren't we, Elvis?" His ears twitch listening to her. "Shall we show Jade how fast you are?" She squeezes him with her heels. They're off.

Dilly and I gallop after them. It's like the past three years never happened.

♀

I'm fixing roast beef for dinner. Scalloped potatoes. Fresh spring peas. Fruit salad.

Toby walks in the back door. Sniffs. "Dang. Did I forget someone's birthday?" He looks over my shoulder. I'm chopping apples. "What gives?"

"Nothing. I just feel like cooking a good meal."

He gets in my face. Stares at me. "You're smiling."

I hold up the knife. "Back off."

"Okeydokey." He backs up slowly. "*Beep. Beep. Beep.*"

Dad and Seth stomp in. "Smells like pot roast," Dad says. He raises his eyebrows.

"Be careful," Toby says dramatically. "She's smiling. And she has a knife."

"Why is she smiling?" Seth asks.

"I don't know. Ask her," Toby says.

"Why are you smiling?" Seth asks me.

I glare at the three of them. "No reason. I'm just happy. Leave me alone."

Dad hangs up his jacket. "If it has something to do with the lotto, remember family comes first."

"I haven't won the lotto." I turn back to the salad.

"Did you get laid?" Toby asks.

"Damn it!" Dad slugs Toby's arm. "She's your sister. Have some respect."

"Ow." Toby rubs his arm. "I thought it was a good question. I'm happy when I get laid."

"Hah! In your imagination," Seth says.

"Both of you get cleaned up," Dad snarls.

"Dinner's in half an hour!" I call. "Then Mom's Skype." I'd told them she wasn't happy with their absence last week. They won't dare sneak out again tonight.

I set the dining table. We only use it on holidays. The boys grumble at first. They're used to eating in front of the TV. But they sit where the food is. Seth and Toby dig in.

"Wait," Dad says. "Maybe we should say grace." He glances at me. As if asking my permission.

I think it's stupid. We never say grace at other meals. I don't think where we eat makes a difference to God. But it would make Mom happy. So I say, "Sure."

We bow our heads. Dad gives a quick blessing. I shake off the religious guilt. It seems a little easier to do tonight. Because I'm still happy.

We eat. Talk about cattle. There was a late calf born this morning. They're going to start branding next week. Dad asks me, "How's that horse working out?"

"Pretty good," I say.

"You gonna win?" Toby asks. "Bury that pretty McNair face in your dust?'

"Yeah. That's the plan."

"Of course she will," Seth says. "Our Jade's got *balls*."

My fork freezes for an instant in my mouth. I lose my appetite. Then I start clearing the table.

"What's wrong?" I feel Seth studying me. "Was it something I said?" he asks.

"Mom's going to call soon," I say.

"She's right," Dad says. "Help clear the table."

"Are you kidding?" Toby says.

"No, I'm not kidding. Jade fixed a nice meal. Now clear the table."

Mom's call comes in a little after six. She's happy we're all there. I tell her about going to the McNairs'. About borrowing one of their horses. Her forehead wrinkles. "Are you and Amy friends again?"

"I think so," I answer. Three years ago, I gave my family a simple explanation. Amy had new friends. She didn't want to be my friend anymore. Mom always figured Amy thought she was too good for us. I never told her otherwise.

"Do you trust her?" Mom asks. "After all this time?"

I think about it. Answer truthfully, "I don't know."

"Be careful, honey," Mom says. "Don't let her break your heart again."

Chapter 10

Mom's words repeat in my head the rest of the weekend. *Don't let her break your heart again.* They repeat in my head when Amy walks by me in the hallway Monday morning. "Hi," she says.

Mike is with me. Does a double take. "Did Amy McNair just talk to you?"

I nod.

He ducks. "Are pigs flying?"

I don't know what to tell him. Is this a new normal? I don't know. *Don't let her break your heart again.*

Mike and I sit at our tree at lunch. I glance over at Amy. She's with Troy. Holding his hand. They look like they usually do. Like a couple. Taking each other for granted. I'm sure he doesn't know about Jesse. Amy sees me. Holds my gaze. Smiles and shrugs.

I smile back. Mike strokes my arm. I quickly shift my gaze to him.

"How's the pickle horse?" he asks.

"Okay." I tell him about Dilly's bad habit I'm trying to break. That she's doing better. But it will take more work.

"Shouldering." Mike bumps me with his shoulder. "You mean like that?"

"Right. If I were a barrel. And you were a horse."

"A horse named Horsey?"

I grin. Shove him. "Stop it."

"Why? I love making you smile. I'm pretty sure it's why God put me on the planet."

My stomach rolls. One more year, I tell myself. One more year and he'll be gone. Off to college. He'll find someone new.

My phone rings. I pull it out of my pocket. It's Seth. He never calls me. My heart stops. Is it about Mom? "What?" I quickly answer.

"You need to come home," Seth says. "Dad was in an accident." He hangs up.

I run to the office. Tell them why I'm leaving early. Race the truck home. Seth didn't explain what happened. But it can't be that bad if Dad's not in the hospital.

I swerve the truck in front of the house. Rush through the backdoor. No one is in the kitchen. The TV is on in the living room. Dad's sitting on the couch. Resting his leg on the ottoman.

"Hey," he says. He's got a sheepish look on his face. "Sorry to pull you out of school."

"What happened?" I sit next to him.

"Fell off the damned four-by-four. Twisted my ankle. Banged up my arm." He holds his elbow.

"Did you go to the clinic?"

"Nah. Nothing's broken. Thought maybe you could wrap it."

"Me? I'm not a nurse."

"It's what your mom would do."

"I'm not Mom! Why can't Seth or Toby help you?"

"They're busy branding. Which you're going to help with when you're done with me. I'm out of commission."

"Dad. I'm in the middle of school. The rodeo's this Saturday. I need to practice."

"And we're your family! This is our living. The calves need branding. You're going to help."

I close my eyes for a second. "Okay." I go to the bathroom. Paw through the cabinet for the first aid kit.

I pull up his pant's leg. His ankle is red. Swollen. Reminds me so much of Freddie it's unreal. "You sure it's not broken?"

"I'm sure. I've had broken bones before."

I wrap his leg in an ace bandage. Grab a bag of frozen peas from the freezer. Form it around his ankle.

He points at the first aid kit. "Any aspirin in there?"

I open a bottle. Hand him a couple.

"Thanks," he says. "Grab me a beer on your way out, would you?"

I take a beer from the fridge. Shake it a little. Storm out of the house before he opens it.

Seth and Toby are in the corral. They've managed to herd a bunch of cows inside. There's a fire going. A branding iron in it. I've helped them brand before. Mom has helped too. It's not easy with just two people. Seth has upended a calf on the ground. He's holding its head and front legs.

My brother is strong. But the calf is bucking its sharp hind hooves. Its worried mother bellows a few feet away. Seth tries to get one of his legs around the calf. It's not working.

I jump over the fence. Grab hold of the calf's hind legs. Pull them back. It's a male. He'll have to be castrated.

"Hey, little sister," Seth says. "Glad you showed up."

"How many have you done?" I ask.

"Just got started," he says. "Took us all morning to herd 'em. Dad falling put a crimp in things."

Toby marches over. "Thanks for coming, Jade." He gives the calf a shot of vaccine. Then attaches a rubber band to the base of its testicles. A minute later Toby is back with the glowing-red branding iron. We roll the animal on its left side. Toby presses the iron against its right shoulder. The double D brand sears its fur and flesh. Sends up smoke and stink. It's over in about a minute. We let the calf go. It runs to its mother.

Seth and I sit there. Watch Toby twirling a lasso. Eyeing another calf. We'll help him catch it. Flip it. And do it all over again.

Seth gets to his feet. Reaches his hand down to me. I let him pull me up. "Gonna be a long day," he says. "You okay with that?"

"Do I have a choice?"

He laughs. Shakes his head. "No."

❧

We stop working when it gets dark. Trudge into the kitchen. My muscles ache. I stink of sweat and burnt fur and flesh. The sound of lowing cows echoes in my ears. I know from experience I'll hear that echo all night.

"Hey," Dad says from living room. I look in on him. Doesn't seem like he's moved. But the guys checked on him all day. Helped him to the bathroom. "What's for dinner?" he asks. "I'm starving."

"Dinner? I'm too tired to cook."

His face turns red.

"Dad," I say. "I've heard way too much bellowing today. Do not start in on me."

I go to the bathroom. Stay in the shower until my skin wrinkles. Don't care how much hot water I waste. When I come out, the guys are in the living room. There's food scattered all over the coffee table. Chips. Crackers. Peanut butter. Sliced ham. Salsa. Cans of beer. "Dobbs dinner of champions," Seth says. "Help yourself."

"Thanks." I drop into a chair. Eat until I'm full.

Chapter 11

I don't check my phone until I go to my room. There's a text from Amy. "U ok? Dad ok?"

The school secretary must have blabbed to her about why I left. I text back, "Sprained ankle. Helping w branding. No training w Dilly till Thursday."

My phone rings a minute later. Amy. "That leaves only two days to train."

"I know."

She's quiet a moment. "Okay. See you tomorrow." She hangs up.

I fall asleep. Too tired to think about how rude she is. How she only cares about herself. How right Mom was to warn me to be careful.

∾

Toby shoves me awake. "Get up," he says roughly.

"No," I mumble. It can't possibly be morning yet. I look at the clock. Six. Dang. I must have forgotten to set my alarm. I tumble out of bed. Quick change into my dirty jeans. Flannel shirt.

Smell coffee. Eggs. Wow. The boys cooked breakfast? Mike would be ducking for flying pigs.

Dad's in the living room. His foot propped up. A bag of frozen corn on his ankle. A plate of scrambled eggs on his lap. Toast. Jam.

Amy walks in. Hands Dad a cup of coffee. "Can I get you anything else, Mister Dobbs?"

"No thanks. I'm great." Dad grins. Points his fork at Amy. "You didn't say she was coming over," he says to me. "About knocked my socks off when she showed up."

Amy shrugs. Smiles. I follow her into the kitchen.

"Eggs?" she says. "I made enough for an army. Wasn't sure how many you had, so I brought a dozen from home. Marta will kill me for not asking first. But, oh well."

"What are you doing?"

"What does it look like I'm doing? I'm helping. Sit down." She sets a plate of eggs in front of me.

I don't know what to say. I can't believe Amy McNair is in my kitchen. Cooking. I hear voices outside. More than just my brothers. I jump up. Look through the window over the sink. Amy's Jeep is parked in front. Along with a large pickup truck. Horse trailer. Jesse is on horseback. So are two guys I've never seen before.

"I told Dad what happened," Amy says. "He likes to work his cow ponies. 'Nothing better than cutting calves,' he said." She looks at the wall clock. "Are you wearing that to school?"

School. The extra guys mean I don't have to help with branding today. I look down at my dirty jeans. "No. But I need to take care of the horses."

"I'll tag along."

I scarf a few bites of egg. Head for the stable with Amy. The brisk morning air is filled with the sounds of men shouting. Whistling. Nickering horses. Lowing cattle.

"Thanks." I'm not sure what else to say. I'm still flabbergasted.

She shrugs. "I remembered watching you guys brand one year," she says. "It was such hard work. And with your dad injured. And your mom not here. Now you can go to school. And train Dilly."

"It's really nice of you. And your dad."

We've reached the stable. "So show me Freddie," she says. "I've never met him." Then she sees Misty. "Misty!" she rushes over to her stall. Kisses Misty's nose. "Oh, you wonderful old thing. I've missed you." Misty nods her head. She clearly remembers Amy. The sight makes me smile.

I shovel old hay and muck out of her stall. Amy grabs hay flakes. Throws them into Misty's clean stall.

"This is Freddie." I open his stall. Feel his ankle. It's not so swollen.

"He's beautiful," Amy says. She strokes his shoulder as he eats. "He looks really strong. Intelligent eyes."

I step back. Watch them. I've wanted Amy to meet Freddie since he was born. The first time I rode him, I wanted Amy to be there. After I broke him, I wanted to ride him to her ranch.

"How fast is he?" she asks.

"He's fast." I pour water into their buckets.

"It's weird being here." She looks around. Fingers Misty's bridle. "It's exactly the same. So are you ready?"

"Yeah. I just need to change clothes."

I change. We decide to share a ride to school. Take her Jeep. She turns up the radio. Her favorite country station. She clenches and re-clenches the steering wheel during an ad. Taps her polished fingernails when a song comes on. She sings. Loudly.

I laugh. Amy was always the loud and impulsive one. I was more quiet and calm. Like the day we went looking for Moo and Mack. I'd told her it didn't make sense. The cows in the painting were Angus. My family raised Herefords. But she just barged out of the house. Tugging my hand. "Come on, Jade! I know they're there!"

She's wound even tighter right now.

She looks over at me. Nods to the beat of the music.

"I'd think about this, you know. Almost every school day. Like, Jade and I are neighbors. We should be riding together. What a waste of gas."

"I've thought the same thing."

"So. Here we are." She frowns. Then smiles again. "It's like we have three years of catching up to do. I don't know where to start."

"We don't have to catch up in one car ride."

"No. But … there are things I want to tell you."

I'm quiet. Wait for her to reveal whatever she wants to say. She fidgets with the steering wheel again. A song comes on. "Oh, my favorite!" She turns the volume up. Sings along. It happens to be my favorite too. I sing along with her.

We end up talking about horses. I'm not surprised. It's where we left off three years ago. It's what we have in common. And it's innocent. Like we have nothing more to worry about than rocks in our horse's hooves. Which trail to take. What snacks to pack in our saddlebags.

But Amy and I aren't kids anymore. And our lives aren't that simple.

Chapter 12

Amy parks the Jeep in the school parking lot. Turns off the ignition. We sit there a second. The radio's off. The engine clicks as it cools. She taps the steering wheel again. Takes a deep breath. I wonder if she's wondering the same thing I am. What comes next? Do we hang out at school now? What about lunch? Do I join Claire, Tyler, and Dana? Become a member of Amy's crew?

Part of me wants to. It's the part of me that's craved being in Amy's life all this time. But I don't know if I'm a good fit anymore. I've heard bits and pieces of their conversations over the years. About guys. Clothes. Movie stars. Singers. Town gossip. School gossip. I'm not really interested. That's not me.

And what about Mike? Lunch is the only time we're together. Do I brush him off completely? Finally end it? I don't want to. He's my friend. So different from Amy, but still important. I reach for the door handle. "Don't worry about school," I tell her. "Nothing has to change."

She nods. "Okay. I'll see you after." She must have come to the same conclusion. The two of us being friends is too complicated. But it's still hard to hear her admit it.

She's staring out the windshield. Not making a move to leave. There are a few minutes before the bell rings. I don't know why, but her dad crosses my mind. The rude way he spoke to Jesse the other day. As if he'd been drinking. Was that new behavior? Old behavior I'd never witnessed before? "You said there were things you wanted to tell me," I say. "Does any of it have to do with your family?"

She reaches behind her seat. Grabs her backpack. "I'll talk to you later." She jumps out of the Jeep. I watch as she trots up the steps. Troy is waiting for her. They kiss. Walk into the building.

I get out. Slam the door. Shove my hands in my pockets. Go to my locker.

"Hi, Jade." It's Lily. "You okay? I was worried. You left in such a hurry yesterday."

I'm surprised the news didn't spread all over school. "My dad sprained his ankle. I had to help with branding."

"Oh, yuck. I hate branding. I'm so glad my dad hires hands to help out." We start for class. "They didn't need you today?"

"No. Some guys came over," I say.

"Cool. Did you hear about the barrel race?" she asks.

"I've been kind of busy. What about it?"

"Oh my God." She touches my arm. "You'll never believe it. Megan Wolf's going to compete."

Megan Wolf. She's a top barrel racer. Grew up on the Northern Cheyenne Reservation. Won the state event last year. "But she's pro. And I thought she was going to college in Bozeman. What's she doing here?"

"Guess she's working with a new horse. Wants a small rodeo to try him out. My dad's an organizer this year. He took her application."

Our event is so small, they combine all age groups and abilities.

"Talk about competition," Lily says. "My time will be snail slow in comparison. But I don't care. It will be fun. How's it going with Amy's horse?"

"Okay. Does everyone know about Megan?"

"Probably not. But they will before the end of the day. You know Wyatt."

We walk into English. My stomach flutters. I wanted to win. Now that doesn't seem likely. Plus, Amy was only loaning me Dilly so she'd have competition. Now that competition will come from Megan, not me. I wish I felt confident in our renewed friendship. But I don't.

ॐ

"Do you have tickets?" Mike asks at lunch.

"What?" I'm trying not to stare at Amy. To fathom

each expression on her face. Her body language. Wondering if I still have a horse for Saturday. "You mean for the rodeo? No. I don't."

"I thought maybe you got some as a contestant."

"No way. So you're going?" I ask.

"Of course I'm going! You're my sweetie." He picks up my hand. Kisses it. "I want to see you ride the pickle horse to victory."

I don't tell him I might not be racing.

"I've never been to the rodeo," he says. "This will be my first time."

"You're kidding. I've gone every year."

"So give me a rundown. What should I expect?"

"Horses. Bulls. People in jeans. Cowboy hats. Fried food. There's the parade in the morning. You've been to that, haven't you?"

"Well, yeah. It's only three blocks from my house. Hey, do you want to watch it together? You can come to my place first. I'm sure Mom will bake something."

I think about it. If I still have Dilly, the McNairs will trailer her. Maybe they will bring my tack too. I'll bring my riding clothes. Show up before the race. Maybe hanging out with Mike will keep my nerves in check. "Sure. That would be great."

৯

I lean against Amy's Jeep. There was a Christian Club

meeting after school. Amy's a member. Kids finally filter out of the building. I notice Amy and Troy are walking several feet apart. Not even holding hands. They must have gotten an earful about sex in there. As in not doing it. Ever. Until they're married, of course.

Amy's eyes are downcast when she gets to the Jeep. "It wasn't locked," she says. "You could have sat inside."

"That's okay. I've been sitting all day."

We put on our seatbelts. She slowly drives off. The radio blasts. I can tell she's still thinking about something. She's not tapping the steering wheel.

I decide to get right to the point. "Did you hear about Megan Wolf?"

"Yeah. It's pretty awesome."

"I was wondering about Dilly. Are you still okay if I ride her?"

"Jade." She glances at me. Then back at the road. "I got you help for branding. Came to your house this morning. Made breakfast. What do you think?"

"Okay. Just checking."

We reach the center of Wyatt. Stop at the town's only signal. A pickup makes a left. Crosses in front of us. It's Ray Belcher and Chris Archer, two popular guys from school. Chris rolls down his window. Waves. "Yo, Amy! Rodeo queen!"

Amy laughs and rolls down her window. "I'm not

the queen yet!" The light turns green. She floors it. Still laughing. "Idiots," she says. The wind blows her long hair out the window. It's incredibly sexy. I quickly look away.

She glances at me. "Come on, Jade. Lighten up. You're scowling."

"No I'm not."

"You've been cooped up too long. You need to get out. I've never seen you at a football game. A party."

"My mom's gone. It's just me. I don't have time for anything else."

She pauses. "Okay. Gotcha. Except you didn't go to parties or games before she left."

I shrug. "I like being outside. I like horses. Shooting. I don't like parties."

"How do you know you don't like them if you've never been to one?"

"Mondays. Kids at school whine about their hang-overs. About getting into stupid fights. Driving drunk. Hooking up with someone they wish they hadn't. I'd rather be home."

"With your Neanderthal brothers?"

I don't respond. If I did, I'd have to agree with her. Or I'd have to admit my brothers are never home weekend nights. Because *they're* out partying. Seth and Toby are cavemen. Dad doesn't help either. He's just as bad. I sigh on the inside. And squirm in my seat. "It sounds like your life is pretty perfect, Amy. Like always."

We've reached the highway. Amy shakes her head. "It's awesome, Jade. Friggin' awesome. I wish I could tell you all about it. But I've decided it might break your heart. So I'm going to spare you."

Chapter 13

The sadness on Amy's face almost breaks my heart. She grips the steering wheel tighter. Her knuckles turn white. She's not crying. But she's close to it. She reminds me of the girl who cried on my shoulder three years ago.

"Amy, what is it?"

She forces a smile. "Nothing. Okay? It's nothing." She breathes in and out a few times. "I wish I could talk to you about boys."

"You *can* talk to me about boys."

"But you won't get it."

I roll my eyes. "I'm human, Amy. I get it. And I have a boyfriend. Remember?"

"But he's not real."

"He's real. We're really dating," I say.

"But have you, you know … had sex?"

"No."

She's quiet.

"I know *you* haven't," I say.

She glances at her purity ring. Nervously fiddles with it.
"Or have you?" I ask.

"No."

"But … you want to?"

Amy slows the Jeep. We're at the cutoff for my house. "Shall I take you straight to Dilly?" she asks. "Or home?"

"Home I guess. Then I can drive myself back."

"Suit yourself." She doesn't say another word until she stops in front of my house. "See you in a few."

I open the door. "You can trust me, Amy."

"Okay."

"I mean it. If we're going to be friends again. I'm here for you. I swear."

She doesn't look at me. "Thanks."

I close the door. She takes off.

The familiar shouts and mooing of branding takes my mind off Amy. I step over to the corral. Jesse and the other two hands are still here. Between them and my brothers they're able to finish two calves at a time. One of the guys is on horseback. Separating a calf from the herd. He seems to just be along for the ride, as his horse does all the real work.

I lean against the railing. Admire the horse as she shifts left. Right. Left again. Her eyes focused on the calf. She's a top cow pony. She'll bring a good price when Mr. McNair decides to sell her.

Seth sees me. Wanders over to the fence. "Hey," he says. "We're almost done. Worked through lunch. We're starving."

"I'm going to Amy's. I'll fix dinner when I get back."

"No. I promised the guys a good meal."

"You what? Seth. The rodeo is this Saturday. I *race* this Saturday. I have to practice."

"Well, that still leaves tomorrow. Come on. These guys have worked hard all day. Because of them, you got to trot off to school. Anyway, it's what Mom would do."

"I. Am. Not. Mom! And I'm not your slave. Do it yourself. Or take them to the Wagon Wheel. I'm going to Amy's." I turn to leave.

"Jade." His deep voice sends a chill up my spine. "I'll tell Mom and Dad where you go online. Those sick forums. The chat rooms."

My stomach clenches. I close my eyes.

"Steaks," he says. "Baked potatoes. Like I said. We've worked all day. We're starving."

I walk to the house. Make dinner for six men.

It's dark by the time I've cleaned the kitchen. Collapse on my bed. I text Amy. Explain why I didn't show up. Ask if she wants to share a ride to school tomorrow. I fall asleep waiting for a reply.

I wake up the next morning. Check my phone. Nothing from Amy. Why? What's going on? She opens up. Then shuts down. Is it her? Is it me? I'm trying to be a good friend. Not do anything to make her feel uncomfortable. But she pushes me away.

My mind fast-forwards to this afternoon. One more day to train with Dilly. That's not enough time. But then, it never was. Amy will be riding a horse she's trained on all year. Even on a new horse, Megan Wolf will come in first. I'll be third, at best. The Wyatt annual rodeo will not be a stepping-stone to anywhere. Another year wasted.

I need to get up. Get dressed. Fix breakfast. Tend to the horses. But my head hurts. And I'm cold. I curl into a ball. Will myself back to sleep.

"Jade!"

I open my eyes. Toby looms over me. "Get up."

I roll away from him.

He kicks my bed. "Come on. Seth and I made our own breakfasts. But you need to take care of Dad."

"You do it," I mumble. Then I remember Seth's threat. "Okay. Give me a minute."

Toby's footsteps retreat down the hallway.

"Crap." I lie there a second longer. Get myself out of bed. Do everything I need to do. By the time I get to school, first period is almost over. Mr. Lynch glances at the clock. "I've already turned in attendance, Jade. You'll have to go to the office this time."

I do what I'm told. I always do what I'm told.

"Do you have a note from your parents?" Mrs. Tibbs, the school secretary, asks.

I shake my head.

She sighs. "This is your third truancy, Miss Dobbs. We'll be sending a letter home to your parents."

"Fine."

"Truancy is a serious issue."

"I know."

"Do you? Because you're not acting like it."

The bell rings.

"I'd better get to class," I tell her. I give her a look. "Don't want to be *truant*."

༄

At lunch, Mike keeps talking about the parade. The rodeo. "So I'm thinking of wearing a red plaid shirt," he says. "Or blue-and-white checks. Which is more cowboyish?"

I glance at Amy. She sees me. Quickly looks away. "I may not go," I say.

"What?"

"Yeah. I may not go. I've got stuff to do at home."

"Like what?" He touches my fingers. "Jade. What's going on? You seem sad. Or mad. Or something. Does this have to do with your mom?"

"No." I wish I could tell him about Amy. About who I am. I wish I could get it all off my chest. I guess I can at least tell him about the race. "I haven't had enough time with Dilly. We're not going to win."

He narrows his eyes. "First of all, I don't know why you're so certain of that. But even if you don't win, isn't competing important? Isn't it good experience?"

I shrug.

"If I were in your shoes, what would you tell me? Like, if I was going to the state science fair. And I didn't think my presentation on nanorobots was good enough. Which is ridiculous, of course. It would be fantastic. But would you tell me not to go? That it's not worth my time?"

I don't need to think about it. "No."

"Well." He holds his hands out. Looks at me.

"This is different. I *know* I'm going to lose," I say.

He rolls his eyes. "No. You don't. Unless you have some fortune-telling ability I'm not aware of. Which would be really cool, by the way."

I tug at bits of spring grass struggling through the hard earth. Force myself not to smile. But I feel a little better. "Okay. I get what you're saying."

The bell rings.

"Then I will see you tomorrow, missy. My house, nine thirty sharp. Yes?"

I sigh. "Yes." He pulls me up.

Chapter 14

I make sure things are okay at home. Then I drive to Amy's. What Mike said made sense. I would have told him to enter that stupid pretend science fair. But that doesn't make me any more hopeful.

I walk into the stable. "Jesse?" I call.

"Yeah! Just a sec." He comes out of a stall. Brushes his hands off. "Hi, Jade. I'll get Dilly."

"Thanks."

He comes back a moment later with her. They stop near the tack room. She swishes her tail. Her gray coat shines. She really is a beautiful horse.

"Thought I'd see more of you this week," Jesse says.

"Yeah. Stuff came up." I hold Dilly while he saddles her. I go through my training routine in my head. I may not win tomorrow. But I don't want to make a fool of myself. I want to get as much out of today's training as I can.

"Hey, guys."

Jesse and I both turn. Amy stands in the doorway.

She's wearing a long satin gown. Her arms are bare. The dark blue sets off her wavy blonde hair. Her pale skin. She twirls. Smiling. Radiant. "So what do you think?" she asks. "I'm going to freeze in the parade. But, oh well."

Jesse lets out a whistle. "Wow."

I have to look away. I stroke Dilly's velvet-soft nose.

"You will be rodeo queen for sure, girl," Jesse says.

"What do you think, Jade?" She steps up closer. Just inches away. "Do you like my dress?"

I don't get it. Why is she doing this? Does she realize she's torturing me? I glance at her face. Focus on her eyes. "Yeah. It's great."

She giggles. "You are two of my favorite people in the world. I wanted your opinions. Now I'd better get out of this. Don't want to ruin it before tomorrow." She waves. "See you later!" She strolls away.

"Holy cow," Jesse mutters. "That is one nice-looking girl." He shakes his head.

I don't say anything. Words don't fit around the lump in my throat.

I force myself to focus on training. Either I'm distracted. Or Dilly's forgotten everything I taught her. She's shouldering again. I spend as much time righting knocked-over barrels as I do riding.

We repeat drill after drill. She improves a bit. I end with an easy trail ride. Then lead her back to the stable. Check with Jesse. Make sure he'll be taking her along with Elvis to the rodeo.

৯

I get to Mike's house thirty minutes before the parade starts. Raise my fist to knock. The door swings open. Mike is wearing a red plaid cowboy shirt. Jeans. And white Chuck Taylors. Well, he tried. He presses his finger to his lips. Grabs me. Pulls me inside. Whispers, "Mom's in the kitchen."

He drags me to his bedroom. Closes the door. "We are never, ever alone," he says. "I'm sick of it."

He wraps his arms around me. Kisses me. I kiss him back. He's breathing hard. I'm not. He glances at the bed. Raises his eyebrows.

"No. No way," I say. "We don't have time. Anyway, your parents are here."

He sighs. Lets me go. "I know. But one of these days, okay? Please?"

"Maybe."

"Maybe." He steps back. "Jade. I know I'm not a hunk. I'm not Troy Regan. Or even Ray Belcher. But you like me, don't you?"

"Yes."

"Then why does it feel like I'm more into this than you are? Did someone burn you in the past? Did something traumatic happen in your childhood? I mean, I don't want to say anything bad about your family. But your creepy brothers—"

"God! Mike, no! They've never done anything like that."

He holds his hands up. "Sorry! I'm sorry. That was a stupid thing to say. But I'm crazy about you. And you're confusing the hell out of me. I want to understand what's going on." He takes my hand. "If I can help, I will. I want to."

I shake my head. I could have sex with him. I'm sure it wouldn't be horrible. But it's not what I want. And it wouldn't be fair to either of us. Because there's no future in this. I'm using him. I shouldn't. It needs to stop. Now. I look him in the eyes. Think about how to word it.

There's a knock. "Excuse me, Mike?" The door opens. His mom sticks her head in. "Oh, hi, Jade. I didn't know you were here."

"Hi, Mrs. Price."

"Coffee cake is ready," she says. "Come to the kitchen."

"Thanks, Mom," Mike says. "We'll be there in a sec."

She leaves the door wide open.

"We better go." I turn to follow her.

"Wait." Mike holds my wrist. "You were about to tell me something."

This isn't something I can rush. "I will. Another time."

He sighs. "Yeah. Another time."

☙

I'm nervous. About Mike. About the race. About Amy. I'm

still able to scarf two big pieces of coffee cake. It's warm, crumbly, spicy. Mike's dad wanders in. "Hi, Jade."

"Hi, Mister Price. Are you going to the parade?"

"Yep. Wouldn't miss it."

I wish Mom were home right now. Going to the rodeo. Watching me ride. I don't know if Dad and the boys will bother going. Do they even remember it's today?

Mike and I walk to Main Street. The parade starts at the high school. Heads straight down Main. Ends up at the fairgrounds and rodeo arena. There's not a lot to the parade. A team of palomino horses. The high school band. Floats sponsored by local stores. A few service-club floats. Church floats. More horses. Old cars. A motorcycle club. More horses. The last float carries the three rodeo princesses. They're dressed in matching cowboy hats and dark blue gowns. The same one Amy modeled yesterday.

My breath catches when I see her. Unlike last night, it feels okay to stare. Everyone else is. She's so beautiful my heart aches. She sees me. Waves. Blows me a kiss.

My stomach tumbles. I have to look away.

"That's so cool you guys are friends again," Mike says. He looks at me when I don't say anything. "Jade, is something wrong?"

"Too much amazing coffee cake." I take a deep breath. Force a tight smile.

She's killing me.

Chapter 15

The parade ends. Most of the crowd follows the parade to the fairgrounds. The rodeo starts in an hour. There's a small carnival too. The bars will be busy all day. I have a feeling that's where my family is.

Mike holds my hand as we walk. "Sorry about earlier," he says. "You need to focus on your big race. Not on me."

"I'll talk to you after the rodeo. I promise."

"Okay. Can't wait. At least I think I can't wait. Do you want to go to the carnival? I'll buy you a bunch of tickets. Try to win you a very large stuffed animal."

I decide I might as well. The opening ceremony is a few hours away. The barrel event is toward the end of the day. Hanging around other competitors will just make me more nervous.

Anyway, I like carnivals. The smell of popcorn. Hot dogs. The scary rides. Little kids shrieking and laughing.

A lot of students from school are here. We say hi as we pass them.

Mike does his best to be nice. Charming. Make me laugh. But I can tell he's not totally into it. Probably worried about what I'm going to tell him.

I need to think about this. Figure out what to say. I trust Mike. But I don't know *how* much I trust him. Amy knows about me. Seth and Toby suspect. What if I tell Mike and he lets it slip to someone? Like one of his friends? My life will never be the same. Like this carnival. People will stare. Avoid me. Talk about me behind my back. I'll be the girl who likes other girls. Nothing more.

However I explain it, it means breaking up with Mike. So this is our last date. I've gotten too used to him. I've let myself get too close. Losing his friendship will hurt.

We're in the game arcade. "Ooh, look." Mike is pointing at a booth. A shooting game. I taught him how to use a rifle. We've done some target practice. Went hunting once. Now he brags he's an expert marksman.

I snicker. "Go for it."

He strides over. Slaps a ticket on the counter. "Pick out your prize now, girlie. Because I am going to ace this."

He doesn't ace it. Even after three tries. But he does win a toy necklace.

"Don't worry," I tell him. "These games are rigged."

"I know. But dang. I wanted to impress you." He ties the necklace around my throat. It's a pink plastic heart with a rhinestone in the middle. "One of my first-ever gifts to you. And it's jewelry. Too intimate?"

"No. I like it. Thanks."

The speakers blare in the rodeo arena. The opening ceremony is about to start.

"I'd better go," I say. "Make sure Dilly got here okay."

He walks with me to the arena. I wrap my arm around him. He does the same. Holds me tight. We reach the entrance. "I'll be rooting for you. And the pickle horse," he says. "No matter what happens, you're the best." He kisses me. Walks to the ticket booth.

I watch him for a moment. Then head to the horse trailers parked behind the grandstand. There are lots of trailers. Lots of horses. Even so, it doesn't take long to find the McNairs'. Like their house, their trailer is huge. Holds six horses. Includes plush living quarters. Dilly and Elvis are tied up outside.

Jesse is sitting on a folding chair. Smoking a cigarette. A piece of paper rests on his lap. "Hey," he says.

"Hey." I check Dilly over. Pet her.

"Nervous?" Jesse asks.

"A little. You?"

"Sure. I'm always jittery before riding a bull. And I got a bad one. That's why I'm sucking on this." He offers me his pack of cigarettes.

talk to you." He walks with me the length of the trailer. "Thought I should let you know there's a buyer here from Wyoming. He's interested in Dilly. For his daughter. He'll make a nice offer. *If* Dilly does well today. I know you'll do your best."

"Sure. Of course."

He pats my back. "That's my girl."

Chapter 16

Did Mr. McNair really need to tell me that? Right now? Did he think I wasn't going to try hard enough otherwise?

I step over to Dilly. Press my head against her neck. "Remember what I taught you. Please."

Jesse unties her. Removes her halter. Bridles her. Not because I'm unable do it myself. Mr. McNair is standing right there. I get on. Ride her away from the trailers. Need to find some empty space alone. Where I can warm up in peace. I walk Dilly. Trot her. Canter. Do some figure eights.

The announcer's voice is constant background noise. Then the crowd cheers. The announcer calls the winner of the tie-down roping event.

The barrel race is next. I glance at the arena. Workers are setting up the three barrels.

Lily crosses in front of me. We wave to each other. She looks stiff. Barely smiles. I don't blame her. Going first is nerve-wracking. She lopes her horse to the end of the arena. To an open area outside the gate. Someone must

"I'll see you after." I ride Dilly away from Amy. Need to focus. Even if it's just for a minute. The rider before me knocks over a barrel. Workers have to right it. The dirt is really soft now. It's harder to make a good time.

The workers leave the arena. An official nods. My name blares over the loudspeaker. I take a deep breath. Give Dilly one last pat. Urge her to a lope. Then a gallop.

Everything fades away as we enter the arena. I don't hear the announcer. Or the crowd. It's just me and Dilly and these barrels. We head to the barrel on the right. Approach it from the left. Circle. Close but clean.

Dilly's hind legs power through the thick dirt. I look ahead to the second barrel. Circle it from the right. We're too close. Dilly skims it with her shoulder. Damn. I don't know if it fell.

I'm already focused on the last barrel. This one we take from the right. I pull her out a little wider. It's a clean turn. We race for the line. I glance at the second barrel. It's lying on its side.

Tipped over.

We leave the arena. I pull Dilly to a trot. She's breathing hard. So am I. I pat her neck. "You did great." She twitches her ears. Lowers her head. She knows she made a mistake. Now I hear the crowd. The announcer. He says my time. But it doesn't register. I don't care. The five-second penalty just killed me.

Amy trots over. I don't want to talk to her. Don't want to deal with anything right now. I turn Dilly toward the trailer. Replay the race in my head. Think about what I should have done. How I should have taken that turn.

"Jade!" Amy calls. Then she's next to me. "Even with the penalty, you came in fourth. You posted a fast time."

I shake my head. It doesn't matter. I made a mistake. Knocked over a barrel. Fourth means nothing.

"Mike!" I call again. I step in front of him. Grab his arms. He stops. Looks away. Oh God. He's crying.

"No need to explain," he says. "I get it."

"I'm sorry."

He pulls his arms away. "Why did you lie to me?"

"Do you remember when you first asked me out? I told you I wasn't looking for a boyfriend. Just a friend."

"But you let it keep going. You led me on."

"I know. I shouldn't have. You don't know what it's like. To be what I am. Here. In Wyatt. I'm alone, Mike. Totally alone. You don't get it. Amy doesn't get it. My family doesn't get it. *No* one gets it. I just wanted to be normal. For a little while." Now I'm crying.

"And you chose me as your chump."

"No. You chose me. And I took advantage of you. Again, I'm sorry. But I'm not sorry I got to know you. You've been a good friend, Mike. A really good friend. You've helped me get through this school year. I *so* wish things could have been different."

"Me too." He glances at my neck. I touch the necklace. He meets my eyes. "Like you wouldn't believe." He walks away. Doesn't look back.

I force myself not to follow him.

I stand there a moment. Listen to the crowd cheering in the arena. Bull riding must have just ended. They announce the closing ceremonies. I wipe my eyes. Quickly jog back to the trailer. Grab my saddle. Press my head against Dilly's shoulder. "Sorry I didn't brush you. I can't be here when your owners get back."

Another thing I'm sorry about? My truck is parked in front of Mike's house. I take my time walking. My saddle weighs a ton by the time I get there. Thankfully, I don't see Mike. Or his family.

I drive down Main Street on the way to the highway. Past the 77 Bar. Dad is staggering out. Seth and Toby stumble out behind him. Part of me is glad they didn't see my race. A bigger part hates them for it.

for the house. Amy walks behind her parents. She reaches the porch. Stops. Glances up at Rattlesnake Hill. Like she senses me here. She finds me. Stares a long second. Lowers her eyes. Disappears inside the house.

I send Freddie down the hill. But not for home. It's still light out. Will be for a while yet. We ride about twenty minutes. To the base of another hill. Our makeshift gun range. I dismount. Tie Freddie to a post. Unsling my rifle.

I load ammo. Start firing. Aim at what's still up there from whoever shot here last. Cans. Broken jars. Bottles. When those are gone, I shoot at shrubs. Rocks. I shoot. And shoot. And shoot.

I shoot until my shoulder is sore. My ears are ringing. The sun is setting.

I check the ammo box. Two cartridges left.

I load them. Sit on the ground. Lay the rifle across my lap. Listen to the breeze brush through last year's brown dead grass. A bird calls. A fly buzzes near my ear.

I should think about this. Think about the consequences. But I'm so tired of lying. Tired of pretending. I don't want to do it anymore. It's better this way. Better for my family. They'll never have to know. Or if they find out, I won't be around to shame them. It's better for Amy. She'll never have to see me again. Mike will get over me. Move on. Which was what I always wanted for him. He's a great guy.

Chapter 18

The sky turns yellow as the sun sets. Then orange. Deep blue. I raise the rifle.

"Jade." Mike is kneeling in front of me. What's he doing here? He's panting. Panting so hard he can't catch his breath. He takes the rifle from my hands. Sets it behind him on the ground. "Oh God. Jade."

He's hugging me now. Breathing into my ear. Wrapping me in his arms. "Jade, I'm sorry." He pulls back. Holds my cheeks in his sweaty hands. "Look at me," he says.

I do. Slowly.

"I don't care if you're gay. Or a space alien. You're my friend. I'm never going to stop being your friend. Okay?"

I don't know what to say.

"Okay?" he repeats.

I nod. I think I'm crying.

He gets to his feet. Throws the rifle over his shoulder. Reaches his hand down to me. "Come on. I'm cold. And there's no way I'm riding bareback. You know I'll fall off."

He will.

I untie Freddie. We walk back to my house. It's a long walk. Mike holds me the entire way.

Want to Keep Reading?

Turn the page for a sneak peek at another book from the Gravel Road Rural series: M.G. Higgins's *Finding Apeman.*

ISBN: 978-1-68021-062-0

Convoy's living room wall. This is clearly more than what's legal. I'm nervous. "So, see ya," I say. Head to the door.

"Hey, Diego," he says. "Got a minute?"

"Not really."

"Come on. I want to show you something. You'll appreciate this."

I take a breath. I want to leave. But I'm curious enough to say, "Okay. A minute."

I follow Convoy's wide butt down a long hallway. Turn to the right. He stops in a small room pasted on the back of the house. That's typical for the old houses around here. Lots of add-ons. What's not so typical is what's in the room. Beakers. Bunsen burners. Scales. Chemicals. I glue myself in the doorway. Don't want to get any closer.

"What is it?" I ask, although I have a good idea.

"Meth." Convoy grins. "I'm branching out."

"Is it safe?" The lab looks sloppy to me. Like it could blow up any second.

He shrugs. "It's safe if you know what you're doing."

"Don't you make enough money with weed?"

"There's never enough, son. I'm supporting an ex-wife and four kids. Anyway, how much more trouble can I get into?"

He has a point. But now I'm even more nervous. "I have to go."

"I've got some ready," he says. "Nice quality." He pulls two tiny bags from his pocket. White powder sparkles inside. "Try it. Give one away. Let me know what you think about it."

"No thanks."

"Are you sure? It will sell itself."

"Yeah, I know. I'm just … I'm not into it," I say.

He shrugs. "Suit yourself."

I'm out of there. Convoy's pit bull and Rottweiler follow me down the front steps. I forget their names. I'd pet them, but I haven't figure out if they're friendly or just pretending. I shove the bag of weed into my backpack. Ride my bike down Convoy's gravel driveway to the dirt road.

It rained this morning. The road is muddy and slick. Redwood trees tower over me, filtering out the sunlight. It takes all of my focus not to slide and take a header.

A mile later I reach the paved highway. The forest turns into pastures. I ride past dairy farms. Sheep farms. Goat farms. The cheese factory where my aunt works. Into the town of Seton, where cows, sheep, and goats way outnumber people.

I park my bike next to our duplex. Lock it to the gas meter. I want to keep the bike in my room, but my aunt births a cow (heh) when I get mud in the house.

I head straight to my room. Rummage in the corner of my closet. Toss shoes and my soccer ball off the old wooden toy box. Slide it to across the floor. Pull the sandwich bags and scale out from under a stuffed tiger and

CHAPTER 6

About the Author

M.G. Higgins writes fiction and nonfiction for children and young adults.

Her novel *Bi-Normal* won the 2013 Independent Publisher (IPPY) silver medal for Young Adult Fiction. Her novel *Falling Out of Place* was a 2013 Next Generation Indie Book Awards finalist and a 2014 Young Adult Library Services Association (YALSA) Quick Pick nominee. Her novel *I'm Just Me* won the 2014 IPPY silver medal for Multicultural Fiction—Juvenile/Young Adult. It was also a YALSA Quick Pick nominee.

Ms. Higgins's nearly thirty nonfiction titles range from science and technology to history and biographies. While her wide range of topics reflects her varied interests, she especially enjoys writing about mental health issues.

Before becoming a full-time writer, she worked as a school counselor and had a private counseling practice.

When she's not writing, Ms. Higgins enjoys hiking and taking photographs in the Arizona desert where she lives with her husband.